Kathie Lee Gifford

THE LEGEND OF MESSY M'CHEANY

For Cassidy,
the real Messy M'Cheany. I love you
exactly the way you are.
—K.L.G.

9 8 7 6 5 4 3 2 1
Digit on the right indicates the number of this printing.

Library of Congress Control Number: 2010943498
ISBN 978-0-7624-4137-2

Cover and interior design by Frances J. Soo Ping Chow
Edited by Kelli Chipponeri
Typography: Jheri Curls and Whitney

Published by Running Press Kids
an imprint of Running Press Book Publishers
2300 Chestnut Street
Philadelphia, PA 19103-4371

Visit us on the web!
www.runningpress.com

Kathie Lee Gifford

THE LEGEND OF MESSY M'CHEANY

Illustrated by
Peter Bay Alexandersen

Music by
David Friedman

RP|KIDS
PHILADELPHIA • LONDON

Come on, children, gather 'roun',
And I'll tell you a tale of the worst kid in town.

Now I've seen some bad ones,
from the East to the West,
But when it came to messes, this kid was the best.

(Messy M'Cheany, the messiest kid in town!)

Even back when he was a baby so teeny,
There never was a kid like Messy M'Cheany.

His mother would bathe him, then put him to bed . . .

And somehow he'd wake up with dirt on his head.

(Filthy dirt on his head!)

Yeah, they called him Messy M'Cheany by name.
When he came through the door things were never the same.

In seconds he could ruin a clean kitchen floor,
Spill his spaghetti—then for kicks, spill some more.

Knock over the fishbowl—ah, he didn't care.
And worse, he refused to wear clean underwear!

(Ugh, disgusting!)
(Messy M'Cheany, the messiest kid in town!)

If he threw a Frisbee, it would land in your soup.

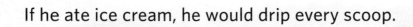
If he ate ice cream, he would drip every scoop.

If he rode his scooter, he'd run over your toes.

He'd toot like a turkey, then he'd pick his nose.

"Look, Ma, GOLD!"

With Messy M'Cheany, things only got worse.
His parents began to think he had a curse.

For wherever he went, he would leave a disaster.
His mother would chase him, but Messy was faster.

(Messy M'Cheany, the messiest kid in town!)

Now Messy thought he was king of the world
Till one day he discovered his world had been "girl'd."

All pink and fluffy and powdered and clean,
She was the strangest thing he'd ever seen!

(Missy M'Cheany,
The Neatest Girl in Town!)

Messy tried to teach Missy how to be dirty,
But she only liked to dress up and be purty.

She'd put on her makeup and dance in her tutu
Till Messy believed she'd completely gone cuckoo.

Then one day just as the sun was goin' down,
Messy faced Missy in the middle of town.
Yeah, they were facin' a real showdown.
Which one would be left still standing around?

Messy kicked the dirt at his feet.

Missy responded by smilin' real sweet.

Messy growled and refused to be nice.

Missy showed mercy
and curtsied—

twice.
(Good girl.)

Messy burped and wouldn't say sorry.
Missy said, "S'cuse me, see you tomorry."
Messy said, "Never."
Missy said, *"Please."*
And that "please" brought Messy to his knees.

"I know I've lived the life of a bum,
But Missy, you've taught me what I could become."

So Messy grew up to be neat as can be . . .

And Missy M'Cheany grew up to be . . . ME!

lyrics

Come on, children, gather 'roun',
And I'll tell you a tale of the worst kid in town.
Now I've seen some bad ones,
    from the East to the West,
But when it came to messes, this kid was the best.
(*Messy M'Cheany, the messiest kid in town!*)

Even back when he was a baby so teeny,
There never was a kid like Messy M'Cheany.
His mother would bathe him,
    then put him to bed . . .
And somehow he'd wake up with dirt on his head.
(*Filthy dirt on his head!*)

Yeah, they called him Messy M'Cheany by name.
When he came through the door
    things were never the same.
In seconds he could ruin a clean kitchen floor,
Spill his spaghetti—then for kicks,
    spill some more.

Knock over the fishbowl—ah, he didn't care.
And worse, he refused to wear clean underwear!
(*Ugh, disgusting!*)
(*Messy M'Cheany, the messiest kid in town!*)

If he threw a Frisbee, it would land in your soup.
If he ate ice cream, he would drip every scoop.
If he rode his scooter, he'd run over your toes.
He'd toot like a turkey, then he'd pick his nose.
Look, Ma, GOLD!

With Messy M'Cheany, things only got worse.
His parents began to think he had a curse.
For wherever he went, he would leave a disaster.
His mother would chase him,
    but Messy was faster.
(*Messy M'Cheany, the messiest kid in town!*)

Now Messy thought he was king of the world
Till one day he discovered
    his world had been "girl'd."
All pink and fluffy and powdered and clean,
She was the strangest thing he'd ever seen!
(*Missy M'Cheany, The Neatest Girl in Town!*)

Messy tried to teach Missy how to be dirty,
But she only liked to dress up and be purty.
She'd put on her makeup and dance in her tutu
Till Messy believed she'd completely
    gone cuckoo.

Then one day just as the sun was goin' down,
Messy faced Missy in the middle of town.
Yeah, they were facin' a real showdown.
Which one would be left still standing around?

Messy kicked the dirt at his feet.
Missy responded by smilin' real sweet.
Messy growled and refused to be nice.
Missy showed mercy and curtsied—
twice.
(*Good girl.*)

Messy burped and wouldn't say sorry.
Missy said, "S'cuse me, see you tomorry."
Messy said, "Never."
Missy said, "*Please.*"
And that "please" brought Messy to his knees.

"I know I've lived the life of a bum,
But Missy, you've taught me
    what I could become."
So Messy grew up to be neat as can be . . .
And Missy M'Cheany grew up to be . . . ME!